For Sara Schotter, always "Passover Perfect"
—R.S.

For Morgan's family
—E.E.K.

Also by Roni Schotter

Hanukkah!

Purim Play

Passover Magic

Also illustrated by Erin Eitter Kono

Hula Lullaby

Little, Brown and Company

Time Warner Book Group

1271 Avenue of the Americas, New York, NY 10020

Visit our Web site at www.lb-kids.com

First Edition: March 2006

Library of Congress Cataloging-in-Publication Data

Schotter, Roni.
  Passover! / by Roni Schotter; illustrated by Erin Eitter Kono.— 1st ed.
    p. cm.
  Summary: Rhyming text describes a family's celebration of Passover.
  ISBN 0-316-93991-9
  [1. Passover—Fiction. 2. Stories in rhyme.] I. Kono, Erin Eitter, ill. II. Title.
PZ8.3.S29734Pas 2006
[E]—dc22

                    2004006989

        10 9 8 7 6 5 4 3 2 1

Book design by Saho Fujii

            TWP

        Printed in Singapore

The illustrations for this book were done in gouache and acrylic paint over a digital collage
on Canson Montval 140 lb. cold pressed paper.

The text was set in Maiandra GD, and the display type is Maiandra GD Demi Bold.

Passover!

By Roni Schotter   Illustrated by Erin Eitter Kono

LITTLE, BROWN AND COMPANY
New York ❧ Boston

When buds burst open and birds appear,
So do our relatives. Passover's here!

Our house looks "Passover perfect"—even Grandma says so.
Everything is sparkly clean, even wiggly Moe!

At the Passover table, Moe gets excited.
He asks if our new puppy Izzy's invited.

"At Passover," Papa says, "no one is turned away.
If Izzy minds his manners, he, too, can stay."

In the kitchen, Mama warms our favorite dish—
Matzoh ball soup! Papa fixes gefilte fish.

Deelish!

Sam adds the special bone to the Seder plate. *Everyone* is busy.
Moe jumps up to sneak a peek. Careful—so does Izzy!

That bone is not
your own, Izzy!

Sundown—time for our Seder to begin.
We hurry to the table. We squeeze and settle in.

Moe sits in a lap to be sure he can see.

Together we read the story of how, now, we are free.

While we sip and dip and eat platefuls of cooking,
Grandpa hides the matzoh—when he's sure we're not looking!

Whoever has the sharpest eyes—
Finds the matzoh and gets a prize!

Is it here? Is it there?
Behind the curtains? Under the chair?

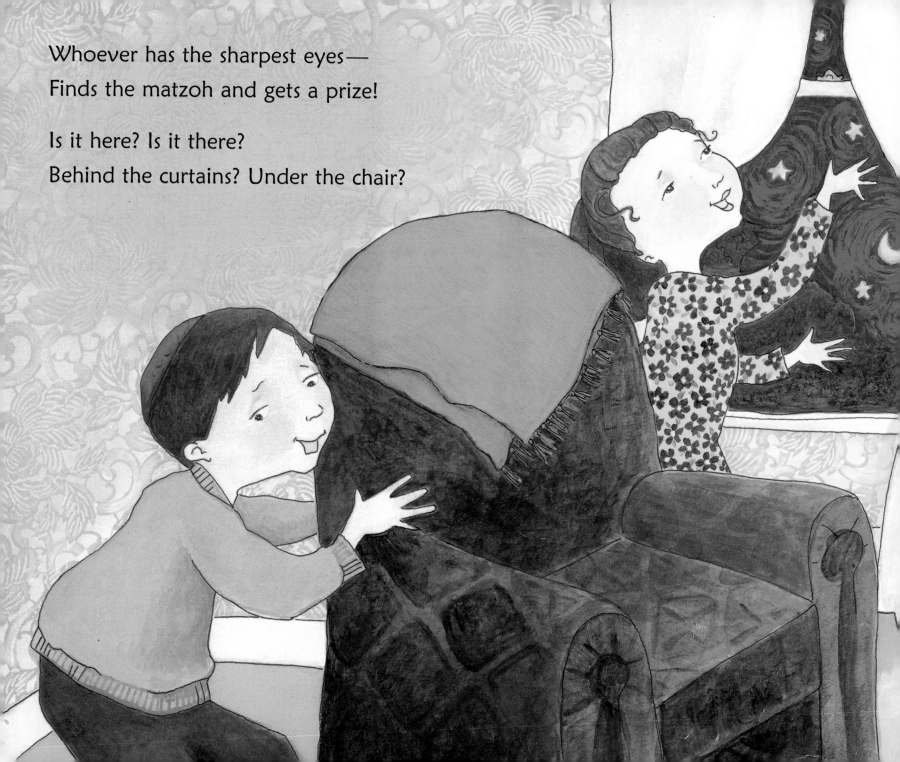

We hunt high. We hunt low. *Where's* the matzoh?
Does *anyone* know?

"Me, me, *me* know!" cries Moe.
He points at Izzy's teeth and gums.
What's left of the matzoh? Only crumbs.
So, can *you* guess who wins the prize?
Moe—the littlest of the guys! Surprise!

Izzy is a matzoh pup.
He loves to eat that matzoh up!

Time to sing songs and to eat *even* more—
While we watch for Elijah and open the door.

We're full now, and fat. We feel cozy and snug.
We reach for each other for a huge family hug.

We're ready for bed. What a long, special day!
We can dream, now, of Passover.
"Yawn. . . *Woof*. . . Hooray!"

During the holiday of Passover, Jewish people feel thankful that they are free and no longer slaves. A long, delicious meal called the *Seder*—with special foods and a special book called the *Haggadah*—helps to tell the story of this freedom holiday. Bitter herbs such as horseradish are eaten as a reminder of the bitterness of slavery. Parsley and other greens stand for life and hope; salt water recalls the tears of the Jewish slaves; a roasted lamb bone recalls the lamb that was used in ancient sacrifices; and a roasted egg stands for that sacrifice and for the promise of new life. *Haroses*, a sweet mixture of fruit and nuts, is the color of the mortar the Jewish slaves used to build buildings for the *Pharoah*, or King, who kept them in slavery. The only bread that is eaten during the eight days of Passover is *matzoh*, the flat bread the Jewish people baked when they were hurrying to escape to freedom and had no time to wait for their bread to rise and become thick. During the *Seder* dinner, a grown-up hides a special piece of matzoh for the children to hunt and try to find. If they find it, they get a prize. Late in the *Seder*, someone opens the door, hoping that the prophet Elijah will appear and sip some Passover wine. People believe that if he comes, slavery, hunger, poverty, and war will no longer exist in the world.

CAN YOU FIND THESE PASSOVER ITEMS IN THIS BOOK?

Bitter herbs, or *maror*

Salt water

Greens, or *karpas*

Haroses

Haggadah

Roasted egg

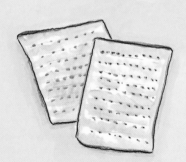

Matzoh

Passover wine

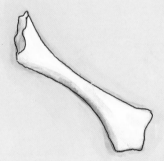

Roasted bone